Guy Bass

LAURA NORDER

SHERIFF OF BUTTS CANYON

With illustrations by
Steve May

To Denise
Who gave Laura her name!

First published in 2019 in Great Britain by
Barrington Stoke Ltd
18 Walker Street, Edinburgh, EH3 7LP

www.barringtonstoke.co.uk

Text © 2019 Guy Bass
Illustrations © 2019 Steve May

A CIP catalogue record for this book is available
from the British Library upon request

ISBN: 978-1-78112-845-9

Printed in China by Leo

CONTENTS

WHO'S WHO IN

LAURA NORDER
the sheriff's daughter

LAURA'S DAD
*the sheriff
of Butts Canyon*

TEN GUN BEN
the outlaw

JEN ERROL
the General Store owner

PORTLY POUNDCAKE
the mayor

MORT L. COIL
the undertaker

BUTTS CANYON

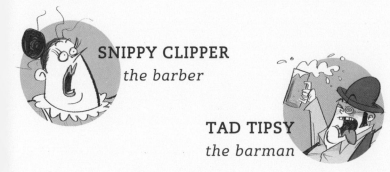

SNIPPY CLIPPER
the barber

TAD TIPSY
the barman

PRECIOUS LITTLE
the gold prospector

HARMONY PLAINSONG
the music teacher

WALTER SPITTY
the bad-mannered man

DOC KNITWELL
the doctor

DUNCAN DISORDERLY
the masked menace

Chapter 1
Welcome to Butts Canyon

A long time ago, before motor cars and microwaves and mobile phones, there was the Wild West! It was an unruly land full of cowboys, cowherds and cowpats. It was a time when men were men, horses were horses and everything else was everything else.

And it was a time of lawless bandits, where the only rule was THERE ARE NO RULES.

Except, that is, in Butts Canyon.

In this small, dusty town, rule-breaking, wrong-doing and bad behaviour were things of the past. In Butts Canyon, there was one lawmaker that no one dared cross.

No, not Portly Poundcake, the town mayor.

No, not even the town's sheriff, who had a badge and an office with a fancy SHERIFF sign hanging above the door.

No, Butts Canyon was run by a ten-year-old girl by the name of Laura Norder.

Laura's only rule was that everyone followed the Golden Rules, a list of dos and don'ts as long as a winding river. And that is exactly what the townsfolk did. But why? Why would anyone do what a ten year old told them to do?

You wouldn't ask that question if you had met Laura Norder.

Chapter 2
Laura Norder Makes a Name for Herself

"Here in Butts Canyon,
we follow the Golden Rules!"

It all began on the hottest Tuesday of the year. The fine folk of Butts Canyon were going about their business. Tad Tipsy the barman poured drinks for thirsty customers, Snippy Clipper the barber cut hair and combed moustaches, and Mort L. Coil the undertaker tended to the needs of townsfolk who were rather less than alive.

That was the day that Ten Gun Ben rode into town.

"Listen up, you no-good, low-down, stinkin', chin-scratchin', dusty-booted, gum-chewin', cow-pokin' cowpokes! I'm Ten Gun Ben, the meanest outlaw since Nine Gun Norris!" cried Ten Gun Ben as he and his band of badly behaved bandits galloped into town. The outlaw went on, chewing on a piece of straw, "If there's a lawman in this town, he'd better run for the hills, unless he wants to meet my ten friends. And I ain't talkin' about the sort of friends you share a campfire with – I'm talkin' about these ten guns that I'm goin' to shoot him with!!"

As it happened, the sheriff was walking his daughter, Laura, down Main Street to school. Ten Gun Ben spotted his shiny sheriff's badge and, quicker than coyotes on a hare, the sheriff and Laura were surrounded.

"T-Ten Gun Ben, welcome to Butts Canyon," Laura's dad said. "H-how can I be of assistance?"

"Time to give up your badge, lawman," snarled Ten Gun Ben, drawing one of his ten pistols. "There's a *new* sheriff in town ..."

"There is?" said Laura's dad. "I hadn't heard! My congratulations to the lucky fella!" He plucked the sheriff's badge off his waistcoat. "Who got the job? They'll be needing this ..."

"No, you dumb bag o' horse feed! I'm sayin' you're finished in this town!" growled Ten Gun Ben. "I'm takin' over Butts Canyon!"

"N-Now, I don't want n-no trouble, Ten Gun," stuttered Laura's dad. Laura saw him shake with fear as Ten Gun Ben's gang circled them like vultures.

"You ain't seen trouble ... yet," said Ten Gun Ben. He hopped off his horse, all ten of his guns clanking and clattering, and strode towards Laura's dad. "Now drop that badge and start runnin' ..."

"Y-yes sir, Mr Ten Gun," whimpered Laura's dad.

Laura watched the sheriff's badge tumble from his hand and drop into the dirt. Ten Gun Ben grinned and bent down to pick up the badge ...

"Hold it!"

Laura's voice was as loud as a howling wolf. Ten Gun Ben and his gang looked down at Laura as she stepped out into the sunlight, dressed in a frilly dress and bonnet.

"Laura ...!" her dad whispered. "What in the name of Aunt Clementine's orange and tangerine pie do you think you're doing?"

"You listen up, Ten Gun Ben. Here in Butts Canyon, we follow the Golden Rules!" said Laura Norder loudly. "And Golden Rule Number Two is – no making trouble!"

"What's Golden Rule Number One?" asked Ten Gun Ben.

"No breaking the Golden Rules, of course," Laura replied.

"*Dangnabbit*, I don't follow no rules!" shouted Ten Gun Ben, taking the piece of straw out of his mouth. "I'm a lawless, no-good so-and-so from dawn 'til dusk. And when I sleep, all I dream of is the rules I'm goin' to break in the mornin'!"

"Mr Ten Gun, sir, my Laura knows you're the toughest outlaw in the Wild West," said Laura's dad. He turned to Laura. "Ain't that right, prairie dog?"

"You ain't tough, mister," said Laura, looking right back at Ten Gun Ben. "I heard you're softer than a bunny rabbit on a goose-down pillow."

"You callin' me soft? That's the last straw!" bellowed Ten Gun Ben. He flicked his straw at Laura and drew another pistol. "I'm harder than the hardest nail, tougher than the toughest cowhide and nastier than a case of belly rot! My only joy in life comes from makin' other folks' lives a misery ..."

"If that's true," Laura began, staring down the barrels of Ten Gun Ben's pistols, "how come you been getting singing lessons off old Harmony Plainsong?"

"How do you know about my singin' less— I mean, what singin' lessons?" Ten Gun Ben blurted.

"I see your sheet music poking out of your horse's saddlebag," said Laura. She pointed to the rolled-up paper poking out of the pocket on his horse's saddle. "You're learning to sing. The sort of sweet, gentle songs a mother would sing to a baby. And 'cause Mrs Plainsong teaches me singing too, I know all about your

8

singing secrets. Sure, you started out sounding like a cat squeezing out kittens, but now you're singing like an angel, is what she says!"

"You shut up about angels!" Ten Gun Ben hissed. He pushed the sheet music deep into his saddlebag. "I got a reputation for bein' meaner than a drunken dentist! This here's the Wild West! If you go tellin' folk I've taken up singin', they won't be scared of me no more!"

"Then I reckon you'd best run for the hills, Ten Gun Ben," said Laura Norder. "'Cause in thirty seconds I'm going to tell this whole town you'd rather be in a sweet singing choir than a law-breaking gang!"

And that was that. The townsfolk watched Ten Gun Ben and his gang gallop out of Butts Canyon. A moment later, a grateful cheer rang out.

"I'm not sure what you did, prairie dog, but you did it!" cried her dad. He picked up his badge, but instead of putting it back on his waistcoat, he pinned it to Laura's dress. "Here, I think this belongs to you," he added proudly.

"You ... you mean it?" Laura said.

"I surely do!" her dad replied. "Why didn't you tell me about those Golden Rules of yours before now?"

"I've been saving them up," Laura said with a shrug. "I've got a whole bunch of them."

"I should hope so too!" laughed Laura's dad. "Your rules saved the day! *You* saved the day!"

The townsfolk stood round Laura and her dad. They patted Laura on the back and told her how plum impressive it was that she'd banished Ten Gun Ben from town. Laura looked down at the badge pinned to her chest and swelled with pride. In that moment, she decided she would live by her Golden Rules for ever. What's more, she decided everyone else would live by them as well.

And that's when the real trouble started.

Chapter 3
The Golden Rules

ONE MONTH LATER

"Golden Rule Number Fourteen! No spitting!
I'm talking to you, Walter Spitty!" cried Laura
Norder. She strode through town and her
sheriff's badge glinted in the scorching summer
sun. Laura wore a wide-brimmed hat and tall
boots. She looked for all the world like her
dad – just half as big. She squared up to Walter
Spitty, a man so dirty that flies buzzed around
him. "We talked about this, Spitty. This is the
last straw!" Laura declared.

"S-sorry, Laura! Bad habit!" whimpered Walter Spitty as he wiped the spit from his chin.

"Maybe the good folk of Butts Canyon will forgive you breaking the Golden Rules if you clean up Main Street," cried Laura, in a voice as loud as cannon-fire. "You clean up every gob of spit, scrap of litter and handful of horse mess. Now get!"

As Laura watched Walter Spitty slink off to find a mop and bucket, she heard a loud "YEE-HAW!" echo across town.

Laura turned to see Precious Little, the local gold prospector, skip into town. She carried a bulging leather bag and had a look of glee upon her face.

"Golden Rule Number Twenty-two – no 'yee-haws' before seven in the evening! Or before seven in the morning, for that matter," roared Laura Norder. She marched over to

14

Precious Little, a tall woman with a big bun of bright blonde hair. "And don't forget Golden Rule Number Thirty-seven! No skipping!" Laura added.

"I-I didn't mean nothing by it, Laura – I'm just happy – happy as a crow with a cool drink of water!" said Precious Little. She opened her bag and showed Laura dozens of nuggets of solid gleaming gold. "I've been prospecting in these parts for years, and I've always come home empty-handed. But today, I finally struck gold!"

"Golden Rule Number Forty – no bragging, boasting or trumpet-blowing!" said Laura, putting her hands on her hips. "Are you trying to make the poor folk of Butts Canyon feel bad about *not* having pockets full of gold?"

"Why, no!" Precious Little insisted. "I didn't mean to brag! I-I would never want to make folk feel lousy ..."

"Well, there's one way to make them feel better – that's by sharing out all the treasure you found," said Laura. "I reckon if everyone gets a nugget, they won't feel so bad after all."

"G-give away my gold?" Precious Little whimpered. "But I spent every penny I had seeking out this fortune. This gold is all I got ..."

"Well, you should have thought of that before you started rule-breaking," Laura Norder declared, grabbing the bag and holding it up high. "Gather round for gold! A nugget for everyone who follows the Golden Rules!"

With that, Laura scattered the gold nuggets on the ground as if they were bird seed, and the townsfolk scraped in the dirt to pick up the pieces. Everyone wanted a nugget of Precious Little's booty. Just then, Laura's dad hurried out of the sheriff's office.

"Laura, what's all this hollering?" her dad said. "Are you forcing your Golden Rules on the townsfolk again? Now look, everyone's just as happy as a horse with a hay bale that you got rid of Ten Gun Ben, but you can't go around ordering folk about like—"

"Hold that thought, Pa," said Laura as she spied a short, round man on the other side of the road. The man huffed and puffed as he tried to climb onto his horse. "Golden Rule Number Forty-eight – no horse hassling!" bellowed Laura, and she marched across the road to see him.

"Laura, wait!" whispered her dad. "That's the mayor, Portly Poundcake! He runs this town!"

Laura Norder rolled up her sleeves.

"Ain't no one runs this town but me," she said. "I've got everything under control."

Chapter 4
Two Words

"You can't be sheriff! You're ten years old!"

"You're too heavy for that poor pony, Portly Poundcake," Laura shouted as Mayor Poundcake tried to get onto his horse. "You'll wear him out before you've even got in the saddle. Ain't no one in this town can trust a mayor who thinks of food before he thinks of anything else. Golden Rule Number Fifteen – no gluttony!"

"Laura ...!" whispered Laura's dad.

"I-I have a healthy appetite, to be sure," muttered Mayor Poundcake, patting his big round stomach, "but that's no reason to be rude ..."

"Maybe if all the horses were better fed, the townsfolk wouldn't care so much that you've been greedy," said Laura. Then she cried out in her loudest voice, "Free hay for every horse in Butts Canyon – and the mayor's paying! Better get baling, Mr Mayor ..."

"But ... but ..." muttered Mayor Poundcake as everyone stared at him.

Laura's dad shook his head as the mayor hurried away to begin baling hay.

"Laura, we talked about this," her dad whispered. "Folks don't much like you sticking your nose in their business. You can't go using your Golden Rules *against* people. It ain't fair."

Laura Norder puffed on her sheriff's badge and polished it up with her sleeve.

"Life wasn't fair when Ten Gun Ben rode into town looking for trouble," she said, "but I sent him packing. You gave me your badge and now I'm the law in this town."

"That was … I was just being nice!" Laura's dad hissed. "You can't be sheriff! You're ten years old!"

"Truth is, there was no order in this town before the Golden Rules," said Laura. "Now everyone knows how to behave. The Golden Rules are the best thing that ever happened to Butts Canyon."

"But there are so many rules, no one can keep up," said her dad. "What if folk get fed up with them? I may not be as smart as you, but I do know this – for every action, there's a *reaction*."

"The Golden Rules *saved* this town! Everyone loves them!" Laura declared. She walked back to the sheriff's office, her arms out wide. "In fact, I'd bet my badge there ain't one person in this whole town who ... doesn't ... love ..."

Laura didn't get to finish what she was saying. Someone had painted two words in red paint on the wall of the sheriff's office. The words were as big as a street sign. They said:

NO RULES

Chapter 5
Duncan Disorderly

*"Why, he's the most wanted bandit
in the Wild West!"*

"No rules?" said Laura. She scowled as she
stared at the words that were daubed on
the wall of the sheriff's office. "Golden Rule
Number Fifty-nine – no graffiti!" She spun
around to face the townsfolk waiting on
Main Street. "Who did this?" Laura shouted.
"Who wrote words where words ain't supposed
to be written?"

One by one the townsfolk gave a shrug or
shook their heads. But Laura spotted someone

slinking through the crowd like a sidewinder snake darting across the desert.

"Hey!" cried Laura. "Hey, you!"

The figure skidded to a halt. He was dressed all in black, with a wide-brimmed hat and a red scarf pulled up over his face. The figure froze, like a cougar waiting to strike.

It was then Laura noticed the figure was carrying a brush and a can of bright-red paint.

"You did it ..." Laura whispered. "You wrote those words!"

The figure dropped the paint can. Then he nodded once and raced away. As he ran, he knocked the hats off a handful of townsfolk before he vanished down an alleyway.

"Get back here!" Laura howled. "Golden Rule Number Two – no making trouble! Golden Rule Number Eleven – no running unless you're late for church or your house is on fire! Golden Rule Number Thirty-three – no masks!"

"I don't think he's listening, prairie dog," said Laura's dad, watching the dust settle. He looked back at the words painted on the wall of his office. "I don't think he likes your rules."

"But everybody knows the Golden Rules are the best thing to happen to Butts Canyon," said Laura as she picked up the paint can. "Who was that masked man?"

"That was *Duncan Disorderly*," wheezed a dry, deathly voice. Laura turned to see Mort L. Coil, the undertaker, limp forward. He was bone thin, as grey as the sky before a rainstorm and looked closer to death than any of the poor souls he buried.

"Duncan Disorderly?" said Snippy Clipper, the barber. "Why, he's the most wanted bandit in the Wild West!" Snippy was small and round but her nose was as sharp and pointy as a pair of scissors.

"Duncan Disorderly lives to make mischief!" added Walter Spitty. "Why, legend has it he's just a legend ... except there he just was, as real as the fleas on my moustache."

"I've never even heard of him," said Laura. "Did anyone get a good look at him, under that mask?"

"I saw him, plain as day!" declared Tad Tipsy, the barman, with a burp. He pushed to the front of the crowd with a jar of beer in each hand. "He's got this long face, a brown mane, swishing tail ..."

"That's Mayor Poundcake's *horse*," groaned Laura. "Tad Tipsy, are you so drunk that you can't even tell the difference between people and ponies?! Golden Rule Number Seventy-four – stay sober!"

"If folk can't get drunk at my saloon, how am I going to make a living ...?" moaned Tad Tipsy under his breath.

"Everybody listen up, there's a new rule in town! Golden Rule Number One Hundred – no Duncan Disorderly!" Laura cried. She pointed to herself with both thumbs. "If any of you see that no-good rule-breaker again, you report him to the sheriff!"

"The sheriff? You mean *me*, right, prairie dog?" asked her dad.

"I reckon it's best if *I* handle this, Pa," said Laura, and cracked her knuckles. She stared out over the horizon as the sun began to set. "I'm going to make this rule-breaking bandit sorry he ever set foot in Butts Canyon. I'm going to teach Duncan Disorderly a lesson."

Chapter 6
Making Trouble

"How can I draw a man when I've never even seen his face?"

As it turned out, teaching Duncan Disorderly a lesson wasn't easy. In fact, if anyone was about to be taught a lesson, it was Laura.

The next morning, Duncan Disorderly struck again. He set all the horses in town free and sent them running to the hills. When Laura stepped out of her house, the horses had gone and the words NO RULES were scrawled into the sandy street in front of her.

At lunch-time, every sign that hung above every store had been swapped around. The townsfolk were in a muddle. They asked Doc Knitwell to give them a haircut and instructed Snippy Clipper, the barber, to examine their boils. They tried to buy cowhide from Harmony Plainsong and singing lessons from Jen Errol's General Store.

Laura found the words NO RULES scratched onto the back of every sign.

Duncan Disorderly struck like lightning. He appeared and disappeared like a shadow. By sundown, Laura was beside herself.

"This is the last straw! Golden Rule Number One – no breaking the Golden Rules!" screamed Laura as she walked up and down the sheriff's office with Duncan Disorderly's empty can of paint in her hands. "How can one person cause so much trouble?"

"I don't know, prairie dog ... but he sure seems to have a bee in his bonnet about your Golden Rules," said Laura's dad, making yet another Wanted poster to stick up around town. "Maybe if we give the rules a rest for a while, he just might leave town ..."

"But without the Golden Rules, Butts Canyon would fall to pieces," Laura insisted. "I'm not about to let that masked mischief-maker run riot. Now, how's that Wanted poster coming along?"

"I'm getting there, but it ain't easy," Laura's dad replied, chewing the end of his pen as he inspected the poster.

"Dang it, Pa, you said you were quick on the draw ..." huffed Laura.

"I was talking about drawing my *pistol*," sighed Laura's dad. "Anyhow, how can I draw a man when I've never even seen his face? Heck, we don't even know if he *has* a face ..."

"Everybody has a face!" snapped Laura. "Just make sure you get all the important details. That big old hat, that mask, those no-good beady eyes ... and draw in this can of paint, too. He was carrying it when ... Wait a minute!"

Laura peered down at the can. The label on it read:

JEN ERROL'S GENERAL STORE
PAINT FOR PAINTING

"Jen Errol makes her own paint and sells it in her store," said Laura. "Duncan Disorderly must have bought this can off her!"

"What does that mean, prairie dog?" asked Laura's dad.

"It means we got ourselves a lead!" Laura declared. She grabbed her dad's Wanted poster and ran out of the sheriff's office with the paint can in her other hand. "Come on, Pa! We're on Duncan Disorderly's trail!"

Chapter 7
Duncan Disorderly Strikes Again

"What's on your mind, prairie dog?"

Laura's dad followed his daughter down the street to Jen Errol's General Store. Laura raced inside to find the leather-skinned Jen Errol, cross-faced keeper of the General Store, which sold everything from soap to horse feed ... to paint.

"Howdy, Miss Errol! How's business?" asked Laura's dad as he hurried into the store after Laura. Jen Errol let out a sigh from behind the counter.

"Why, since your Laura stopped me selling chewing gum I've almost gone *out* of business," Jen Errol huffed. "Everyone was plum crazy about that candy – it sold like hot cakes ... unlike my hot cakes."

"Golden Rule Number Ninety-six – no chewing on nothing that ain't actual food ... but gum ain't why we're here," said Laura. She slammed the empty paint can down on the counter. "Who did you sell this paint to? There's no way Duncan Disorderly could have strolled in here wearing a mask – you'd have remembered him. So the way I see it, you *must* have seen his face when you sold him this paint."

"I ain't seen any new faces," said Jen Errol with a shrug.

"Well, that settles that," said Laura's dad with a shrug. "We'll leave you in peace, Miss Errol ..."

"Now, hang on," insisted Laura. "Somebody purchased this paint. And it had to be a stranger, unless – wait a minute!"

"What's on your mind, prairie dog?" Laura's dad asked.

"Think about it, Pa," Laura said, her eyes wide. "If it wasn't a stranger bought this can of paint, then it must have been someone Miss Errol knew. It must have been one of the *townsfolk*."

Jen Errol froze.

"I-I didn't say that! I didn't say that!" insisted Jen Errol.

"You didn't have to," Laura said, and she glowered at Jen Errol.

"I don't understand," said Laura's dad.

"I've got a hunch Duncan Disorderly is someone from right here in Butts Canyon," Laura replied. "One of the townsfolk is breaking the Golden Rules, even though they're the best thing that's ever happened to—"

"*AAAAAAH!*"

The scream came from outside. As quick as a flash, Laura grabbed her paint can and Wanted poster and rushed into the street.

"Duncan Disorderly has struck again!" came a cry. There was Harmony Plainsong, rolling on her back in the middle of the street. She was so round and helpless that she looked just like an upturned beetle.

"Mrs Plainsong! What happened?" Laura cried as she and her dad helped Harmony Plainsong to her feet.

"Why, it was Duncan Disorderly!" Harmony Plainsong declared. "He stole my shoes! He stole all our shoes!"

Laura looked down at Harmony Plainsong's feet. Sure enough, her shoes had gone and she was in her stockinged feet. Laura looked right, down the street. Another twenty or so townsfolk had been knocked down, and they had all had their shoes stolen.

"Laura, look!" cried Laura's dad. Laura looked left. There, in the middle of the street, as clear as a fly in a bowl of soup, was Duncan Disorderly. He stood there proudly, his arms outstretched – and at his feet were the stolen shoes, all carefully arranged on the ground so as to spell out two words:

NO RULES

"Duncan Disorderly, you're under arrest!" Laura bellowed. Duncan Disorderly nodded and touched the brim of his hat. Then he darted

into an alleyway. Laura roared in anger. "Rule Number Twenty-nine – no fleeing the scene of a crime! You get back here, you no-good, low-down rule-breaker!"

Chapter 8
Nowhere to Run

"Why, that Duncan Disorderly is faster than a rattlesnake and sneakier than a bobcat ..."

Laura broke into a sprint. She raced down the alleyway, with her dad hot on her heels. Laura saw Duncan Disorderly vanish round a corner.

"There's nowhere to run, Duncan!" Laura cried. "You can't reach the hills without a horse and—"

"Laura! Look!" her dad yelled from behind her. Laura spun around. There, at the other end of the alleyway, stood Duncan Disorderly.

"What the ... It isn't possible!" Laura cried. "He was ahead of us! How did he get *behind* us?"

Laura and her dad high-tailed it back down the alleyway. And as they came out into the street, there was Duncan Disorderly hurrying between Snippy Clipper's barber's shop and Mort L. Coil's undertaker's. Laura raced after him.

"Get back here!" she cried, panting as she ran. She'd almost reached the other side of the street when her dad yelled again.

"Laura! Up there!"

Laura spun around and looked up. Racing along the roof of the barber's shop was Duncan Disorderly.

"How'd he get up there?" Laura declared. "Not even a dang vulture could get so high so fast!"

42

By now Laura was almost out of breath, but she wasn't about to give up. Duncan Disorderly had no choice but to climb down the other side of the building.

"There's nowhere to run, you bad-to-the-bone bandit!" Laura cried as she ran round the corner of the barber's. "I've got you no— AAH!"

Laura threw herself to the ground as a horse galloped out from the side of the building – with none other than Duncan Disorderly in its saddle. By the time Laura knew what was happening, Duncan Disorderly was halfway to the hills, leaving a trail of dust behind him.

"Stop! I haven't taught you a lesson yet!" Laura howled as her dad hurried over and helped her to her feet.

"Why, that Duncan Disorderly is faster than a rattlesnake and sneakier than a bobcat ..."

her dad said. He picked up her hat, which had flown from her head when Laura leaped out of the horse's path. "This feels like it's getting out of hand. Maybe we should give him what he wants and give up the rules for a—"

"This is the last straw!" Laura interrupted, ignoring her dad. She dusted off her hat and pushed it onto her head. "I'm *through* chasing Duncan Disorderly … I've got a new plan."

"What are you going to do, prairie dog?" asked Laura's dad.

"I'm going to find out who he is under that mask," said Laura. "And I know just where to start."

Chapter 9
Everyone's a Suspect

*"I'll bet my badge one of you is
Duncan Disorderly!"*

Laura sent her dad back to the sheriff's office
to work on more Wanted posters and made her
way to the local saloon. She ducked under the
saloon's swing doors and pushed inside. She
held the empty can of paint in her hand and
she had a Wanted poster under her arm.

The bar was bustling with townsfolk.
Precious Little ... Mort L. Coil ... Walter Spitty ...
even Portly Poundcake, the mayor. Laura's
eyes darted around the room as she climbed up
onto a barstool.

"Give me a glass of milk," Laura said as she plonked the poster and the paint on the bar. Tad Tipsy, the barman, quickly poured her a glass of milk and slid it across the bar towards her. Laura grabbed the glass and swigged the milk in one go.

"Another," she growled.

"Now look here, Laura, we don't want any trouble," said Tad Tipsy, refilling her glass.

"You ain't seen trouble ... yet," Laura said, swigging the milk. She wiped her mouth with her sleeve. Then she slapped her hand onto the Wanted poster. "Y'all might have heard I just had a run-in with Duncan Disorderly. Y'all know that I'm looking for him. Y'all know I ain't caught him yet. But what y'all don't know is *I* figured out something ... I figured out Duncan Disorderly is one of *you*."

"One of us? Now hang on a minute," said Portly Poundcake. "You're surely not

suggesting one of the townsfolk is that brazen rule-breaker ..."

Laura picked up her glass of milk and raised it to her lips.

"No, I can't afford to get sleepy – got to stay sharp," Laura said to herself, and she pushed the glass away. She hopped off her stool and began to march around the bar, glaring at one person after another. "Truth is, you all had reason to turn against me. Walter Spitty, I made you clean up the streets for spitting ... Precious Little, I made you give up your gold ... Mayor Poundcake, I pointed out what a big old slice of pie you are! All of you got reason to hate the Golden Rules. I'll bet my badge that one of you is Duncan Disorderly!"

"You can't rightly suspect one of us is the most wanted bandit in the Wild West!" gasped Precious Little.

"Especially since most of us were there when you first set eyes upon Duncan Disorderly," added Walter Spitty.

"I-I can't fathom it, but I know it's one of you! I know it!" said Laura. She picked up the paint can and waved it at them. "One of you is Duncan Disorderly, and I ain't going to stop until I find ... out ... who..."

Laura trailed off as a low rumbling sound filled the air. She looked back at the bar and saw her milk start to ripple in its glass. In moments, the whole saloon began to shake as if caught in an earthquake. Laura raced out of the saloon doors into the street.

The air was thick with billowing, blinding clouds of dust. Laura turned to her right and squinted up the street. Huge dark shapes were moving quickly towards her. *Horses?* Laura thought. *No ... buffalo!*

Laura was right. A herd of wild buffalo was charging into town ... and they were headed straight towards Laura.

Chapter 10
The Last Straw

"You're Duncan Disorderly?"

"Stampede!" Laura cried as the herd of buffalo charged through Butts Canyon, crashing through porches, knocking down street signs and breaking rules all over the place. Laura knew that if she didn't move, she'd be flattened. She screamed and leaped onto a hay cart, up onto the highest bale, as the buffalo ran past. The cart shook and swayed as the great beasts ploughed onwards through the town.

"What in the world could have made them trample through town?" Laura screamed.

That was when she saw the figure on horseback, riding slowly through town behind the buffalo stampede. As the billows of dust began to clear, Laura noticed he was dressed all in black, with a large hat and a red mask.

"Duncan Disorderly!" yelled Laura. "It was you! It was you who spooked the herd! Golden Rule Sixty-one! No buffalo-bothering!"

Duncan Disorderly trotted slowly by on his horse, saying nothing. "What do you want me to say?" Laura roared. "Do you want me to say you made a fool of me? Tell me what you want!"

The mysterious masked man touched the rim of his hat as he rode past and said, in a voice as dry and coarse as a desert wind:

"No rules."

With that, Duncan dug his spurs into his horse's flanks and it broke into a canter. Laura sank to her knees in the hay.

"No rules! Always 'no rules'," Laura groaned. Maybe her dad was right – maybe the only way to stop Duncan Disorderly was to give him what he wanted. Every time she tried to enforce the Golden Rules, Duncan Disorderly just made more trouble for the town. What if he never stopped?

For a long moment, Laura watched Duncan Disorderly gallop across the plains, kicking up dust from a desert that couldn't care less about the trials and troubles of human folk. Laura felt deflated and defeated. She felt as if Duncan Disorderly hadn't just beaten her ... he'd beaten her Golden Rules.

Laura sighed. She picked a piece of straw out of her hair and stared at it. She remembered banishing Ten Gun Ben from Butts

Canyon. It had made her the most important person in town.

Imagine if I banished Duncan Disorderly, too, Laura thought. *It'd make me the most important person in the whole Wild West!*

"No ... No, I *ain't* giving up. This is the last straw!" Laura said aloud, and leaped to her feet. She saw Portly Poundcake's horse tied up outside the saloon. Laura leaped onto its back and set off. "Duncan Disorderly, hold it right there!" she cried. "I ain't finished with you!"

Laura gave chase. She wasn't a skilled rider, but Mayor Poundcake's horse was so pleased to have a lightweight rider on its back that it broke into an impressive gallop and quickly gained on Duncan Disorderly. Duncan looked back and spurred his horse on again, drawing away from Laura as he headed for the hills. In moments, he'd be free again. Laura shouted after him – and then noticed that she was still carrying the bandit's empty can of paint.

"Hey! You left this in the street!" Laura bellowed, pulling back her arm. "Golden Rule Number Seventeen – no littering!"

With that, Laura hurled the paint can as hard as she could. It flew through the air in a perfect arc, until:

CLONK!

The paint can struck Duncan Disorderly on the back of his head, knocking him off his horse and sending him grinding into the dust.

"Yes!" cried Laura as she tugged on her horse's reins and dragged it to a halt. She hopped down from her horse and raced over to Duncan Disorderly, who writhed and groaned in the sand. Laura grabbed the bandit's mask and pulled it down.

"I've got a new Golden Rule – no messing with Laura Nor ... *Dad?*"

Laura couldn't believe her eyes, but there, under the mask, as clear as water from a well-spring, was her dad.

"I-I'm sorry, prairie dog," her dad groaned. "I didn't know what else to do ..."

"I don't understand," Laura muttered, stumbling back. "It was *you* all along? *You're* Duncan Disorderly?"

"Your father is not Duncan Disorderly," said a voice. Laura turned to see a small army of black-clad figures. There were thirty of them at least, all dressed in the same wide-brimmed hats and red masks. Wherever Laura looked, there were Duncan Disorderlys.

"What's going on ...?" Laura whimpered. One of the Duncan Disorderlys stepped forward with a distinct limp and pulled his mask from his face. It was Mort L. Coil, the undertaker. Another Duncan Disorderly stepped forward and removed her mask – she was Precious Little, the gold prospector. A third did the same, and Laura saw the face of Jen Errol, the owner of the General Store. Soon, all the Duncan Disorderlys had removed their masks. Walter Spitty ... Snippy Clipper ... Tad Tipsy ... Harmony Plainsong ... Doc Knitwell ... even Portly Poundcake, the mayor.

"We are all Duncan Disorderly," said Mayor Poundcake. "All of us."

Chapter 11
Laura Learns a Lesson

"Maybe you're too good for your own good."

"Laura, I'm sorry," Laura's dad said again as he dragged himself up from the desert sand. "But it's true, we're *all* Duncan Disorderly."

"We all dressed up as him so we could create as much trouble as possible," explained Precious Little.

"You thought you were chasing just *one* Duncan Disorderly around town, but in fact it took all of us to outrun you," said Tad Tipsy. "One in the street, another in the alleyway, another on horseback ..."

"Heck, I nearly broke my neck climbing up on that roof!" added Snippy Clipper.

"See, the townsfolk just got plum sick of all your dang rules," Laura's dad explained. "They were fixing to run you out of town."

"*Run me out of town?*" Laura gasped. "But … but the Golden Rules are the best thing that ever—"

"That ain't how the townsfolk see it," interrupted Laura's dad. "They think the power might have gone to your head."

"Might?" howled Mayor Poundcake. "Laura Norder, your Golden Rules have created a moral compass that's impossible to live by, and you've upset everyone in Butts Canyon!"

"I managed to convince the townsfolk they didn't have to kick you out," said Laura's dad. "I figured if you finally met someone who

wouldn't follow your rules, you might give up –
and we might get to stay in Butts Canyon."

Laura felt herself go weak at the knees.

"I-I thought y'all liked the Golden Rules,
especially since *I* liked them so much," Laura
confessed. "But I guess if you hate them enough
to make you do all this, *maybe* I can give them
up ... if it means you won't run me out of town
and all."

"You're a good girl, Laura," Laura's dad said,
putting his arm around her. "In fact, maybe
you're too good for your own good."

*

As the crowd of townsfolk moved away, Laura
watched the sun begin to dip behind the
horizon. Maybe, just maybe, she'd let her love
of the Golden Rules get a little out of hand.
She looked down at the sheriff's badge pinned

to her waistcoat. Then she unpinned it and polished it with her elbow.

"I guess this is yours, Pa," Laura said as she handed the badge back to her dad. "I reckon it's time for a change."

"Thanks, prairie dog," said her dad, returning the badge to his lapel. "Maybe we get you a *deputy's* badge instead, what do you say?"

"I don't think so … I sure don't like the idea of being run out of town," Laura admitted. "I guess I'll have to find myself something else to do. I just ain't sure what …"

"You're the girl who made Ten Gun Ben run for the hills," said her dad, giving Laura a hug. "You can do *anything* you put your mind to."

As Laura's dad hugged her tightly, Laura looked down at her dad's mask and hat, lying in the dust. An idea began to form, and a smile spread across Laura's face.

"Golden Rule Number One Hundred and One," she whispered to herself, picking up the mask. "There are no rules."

The End ...?

Our books are tested
for children and young people by
children and young people.

Thanks to everyone who consulted on
a manuscript for their time and effort in
helping us to make our books better
for our readers.